Published in North America in 2016 by Owlkids Books Inc.

Originally published in France under the title *Marlène Baleine* in 2009 by Éditions Sarbacane.

Owlkids Books acknowledges the financial support of the Canada Council for the Arts, the Ontario Arts Council, the Government of Canada through the Canada Book Fund (CBF) and the Government of Ontario through the Ontario Media Development Corporation's Book Initiative for our publishing activities.

Published in Canada by
Owlkids Books Inc.
10 Lower Spadina Avenue
Toronto, ON M5V 2Z2

Published in the United States by
Owlkids Books Inc.
1700 Fourth Street
Berkeley, CA 94710

Library and Archives Canada Cataloguing in Publication

Calì, Davide, 1972-
[Marlène Baleine. English]
   Abigail the whale / written by Davide Cali ; art by Sonja Bougaeva.

Translation of: Marlène Baleine.

Translated by Karen Li.

ISBN 978-1-77147-198-5 (hardback)

   I. Bougaeva, Sonja, 1975-, illustrator II. Li, Karen, translator III. Title. IV. Title: Marlène Baleine. English.

PZ7.C1283Ab 2016   j843'.92   C2016-900397-3

Library of Congress Control Number: 2016930946

Manufactured in Shenzhen, Guangdong, China, in April 2016, by WKT Co. Ltd.
Job #15B3279

A   B   C   D   E   F

Publisher of Chirp, chickaDEE and OWL   Owlkids Books is a division of Bayard CANADA
www.owlkidsbooks.com

ABIGAIL THE WHALE

Written by Davide Cali   Art by Sonja Bougaeva

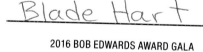
Owlkids Books

Wednesday was swimming day.

Abigail left the change room and squirmed past the shower, trying to avoid the icy water. Then she counted her way to lane seven.

Abigail always tried to be last in line, because she knew that when she dived in, she would make an enormous wave, and everyone would shout,

"ABIGAIL IS A WHALE!"

Abigail hated diving. She also hated swimming. She hated all the strokes:

front crawl, **backstroke,** **breaststroke,** **butterfly.**

She felt like she caused a tsunami every time she moved. She was big.
And all the other kids teased her, saying,

"ABIGAIL IS A WHALE!"

When class was over, the swimming teacher talked to Abigail.

"What's wrong, Abigail? Don't you like swimming? You're a good swimmer, you know."
"No, I'm too big and heavy."
"That's not true. That's just what you *think*."

What was he talking about?

"We are what we *think*," her teacher said. "If you want to swim well, you have to *think light*. Do you suppose birds or fish *think* they're too heavy? Of course not!

"So if you want to *feel light, think light!* Try it!"

That's a funny idea, thought Abigail, but I'll try it.
And in the shower, she closed her eyes and began to *think water*.

water

water

W-A-T-E-R

It was strange. Maybe it was just this shower, which for once was hot,
but suddenly Abigail felt liquid . . . as if she were made of flowing water.

By the time Abigail left the pool, it was already dark. Her house wasn't far, so she was allowed to walk home alone. But sometimes the dark made Abigail feel small and scared.

Tonight, Abigail *thought big.*

She *thought*

giant!

It worked!

It was a brilliant idea. Later, in bed, Abigail *thought* of a

hedgehog

in its burrow, ready to sleep through the winter.

Quick as a wink, she was deep asleep.

All week, Abigail followed the swim teacher's instructions.

She *thought*
kangaroo.

She *thought*
statue.

She *thought*
rabbit.

She *thought* of the shining sun.

And it worked!

She jumped high in gym class.

She didn't feel the sting when she got a needle.

She ate all her carrots at lunch.

And Elliot smiled at her for the first time ever . . .

The following Wednesday, Abigail stepped out of the change room.
She *thought*

Stone

so that she wouldn't feel the icy shower. Then, as usual, she
walked to lane seven. Abigail got in line and waited her turn
to dive. Then she *thought*

rocket

and entered the water without a splash.

Abigail *thought* light.

Abigail *thought*

sardine,

eel,

barracuda,

shark.

And then . . .

Kayak . . . and she swam the front crawl.

Surfboard . . . she swam the backstroke.

Submarine . . . she swam the breaststroke.

Speedboat . . . she swam the butterfly.

"Way to go, Abigail!"

All the kids in the class were watching.
This time, no one shouted, "Abigail is a whale!"
But one of them, Betty, said, "You're such
a good swimmer now, you should jump from
the high diving board!"

Abigail knew that Betty didn't think she was brave
enough to jump from such a height. Abigail climbed
up, up, up, to the diving board. She looked at the water.
Abigail *thought*.

She *thought very hard*:

whale.

No, even better . . .